lunar savings time

lunar savings time

stories

by Alex Epstein

translated from the Hebrew by Becka Mara McKay

clockroot books

To my parents

First published in the United States in 2011 by

Clockroot Books
An imprint of Interlink Publishing Group, Inc.
46 Crosby Street
Northampton, Massachusetts 01060
www.clockrootbooks.com

The poem by Jovica Ivanovski quoted in "On Dead American Poets and Social Networking" is translated by Elizabeta Bakovska, and used with permission of the poet.

We gratefully acknowledge the following publications, in which some of these stories have appeared: the *Kenyon Review Online*, the *Iowa Review Online*, the *Collagist*, and *Electric Literature*.

Library of Congress Cataloging-in-Publication Data

Epshtain, Aleks, 1971-
[Kitsure derekh ha-baitah English]
Lunar savings time / by Alex Epstein ; translated by Becka Mara McKay.
  – 1st American ed.
    p. cm.
Includes bibliographical references.
ISBN 978-1-56656-852-4 (pbk.)
I. McKay, Becka Mara. II. Title.
PJ5054.E597K5813 2011
892.4'36–dc22
                                            2011011643

Printed and bound in the United States of America

Front cover image copyright © Jwohlfeil | Dreamstime.com
Book design by Juliana Spear

spring is like a perhaps
Hand in a window

e.e. cummings

Contents

On the Power of Russian Literature

My great-grandmother once shut a book by Tolstoy so hard that a spark came from its pages, and the spark climbed up the curtains, and ignited a fire, and our summer house went up in flames. I did not inherit this talent of my great-grandmother's, but once I did try to write a story in which everything took place in reverse: the summer house goes up in flames, the curtain burns, a spark catches in the pages of *Anna Karenina*, and so on: my great-grandmother shut the book so hard that the fire was extinguished.

Rain Is Stronger than Death

"What is stronger than me?" asked Death. The boy answered, "Rain." "And what is weaker than me?" asked Death. The boy answered, "Me." "So you know why I'm here," said Death. "I know," said the boy. "To fulfill my last wish." "And what is it?" asked Death, cautioning, "Just remember that you can't ask for dozens of wishes." The boy, who wanted to walk again in a forest of ten thousand trees, and fall asleep in one room and wake up in another, and just one more time hold his father's razor, said, "I want you to ask me another question." "What is equal to me?" asked Death. The boy said, "A story."

A Small Lexicon of Lullabies

And it was summer. The ghost was a young pregnant woman. And it was autumn. Once it was a little colder, and the maple trees grew a little slower. Stradivarius, they say, used to make violins out of them. And it was winter. The Zen monk updated his Facebook status: "In the evening it snowed. In the night I dreamed it was snowing." And finally, spring: the ghost's water broke.

How the iPad Saved the Short Story

The truth of the matter is that the iPad did not save the short story, and in any case this was not the reason that one man, fed up with his life, jumped from the window of his apartment on a high enough floor. And then, in the middle of the journey to the sidewalk, he suddenly discovered he could actually fly. He began to hover above the city streets, and flew up and down and forgot that he had just jumped from the window to die, and even cautiously approached the utility lines (without which the world is demilitarized from sadness). After a few minutes, when he turned in the general direction of his window, he could no longer fly. He started to fall, managed only to think he should ascend one last time, but it was no use, he spun through the air, plummeting and crashing on the road just a few minutes' walk from his home. What a brief and bizarre kind of grace this was. But grace nonetheless.

Closer to the Rain

The instructor of the photography workshop says that in a few years, digital video will be of such high quality, and the processing power of cameras so much greater, that we'll simply capture everything on video, and take the still photos that we want out of the footage. The man who received the course as a gift from his children recalls: the first time that he and his wife traveled abroad together, the weather in Rome was a complete disaster. After the fourth umbrella they bought from a street vendor had broken within an hour, they returned to their hotel and asked the concierge to take their picture in front of a white wall. This was a long time before the age of Photoshop. They had to use the good old-fashioned method of scissors and glue with the postcards they bought at the airport. ("But all of this," says the instructor, "is in the future." Meanwhile, in the studio's perfect light, he is about to demonstrate the position of the macro mode that every digital camera has: he places a pot of geraniums on a tall chair.) If only he could sort out all of these little stories and decide which was best to remember.

The Book of Sleep

This story is somewhat familiar: On the seam of the seventeenth and eighteenth centuries, the Orientalist Antoine Galland translates *The Thousand and One Nights* into French, and weaves in legends and tales of Scheherazade that he invented himself, or that he'd just heard during his travels in the East (like the one, for example, about Aladdin and the magic lamp). In Galland's journals, by contrast, in an adaptation by the Argentine writer Bioy Casares, we encounter another story, which Galland actually avoided including in his translation of *The Thousand and One Nights*: He states that at a market in Toulouse he obtains a tattered book that was said to have been written by a gypsy. Whoever reads from this book from dawn until dusk, the bookseller instructs Galland, will fall asleep and awaken after one hundred years. Only then will he continue to read the book at the exact place he'd stopped, without knowing that the world outside is unrecognizably changed (again). Galland returns home and one morning begins to read the book as instructed. At night he falls asleep and awakens the next day: a lazy autumn in the south of France. The only thing that happened, he recalls through the curtain of waking, was that also in his dream he'd slept and awakened from another dream, and it isn't clear to him which of the two dreams is real. Galland copies into his journal one of the opening lines from the book, "The god prayed. But to which god? Thus is the universe made," and then places the fraudulent book in his library, and returns to the labor of translating

The Thousand and One Nights. Elsewhere in his journal he remarks that perhaps it isn't the man who sleeps for one hundred years, but the book.

Three Pieces of Time

1

A year ago, in a small town in the United States, I saw a beggar sitting beside a cardboard sign that read: "Help me: my time machine is out of order. I need money for replacement parts, so I can go back home, to 2118."

2

To accept the assumption that God created the world less than six thousand years ago, one must accept the claim that He also created signs and traces of everything we assume happened before that: dinosaur skeletons, continental drift, cave paintings, and so on. In one of his essays, Borges quotes Russell, who writes that in the same vein one can argue that the world, with its entire glorious past, was created a few minutes ago. A more radical idea is found in a Zen parable from which I copied the next lines: A teacher was asked by one of his students when the world was created. He answered, "Now."

3

The legend goes that Virgil wrote the *Aeneid* for ten years, no more than three lines each day. And at the end of his days he began subtracting from his poem: Among the lines he was satisfied to leave out was one of the tales of Aeneas, who wanders and wanders the streets of Carthage, until he comes to a square bustling with people. He pushes his way into the crowd and listens to a blind storyteller, who tells of the journeys and hardships of a man who cannot find the way home—Odysseus is his name. "But not even a single road leads out of Troy!" cries Aeneas, perhaps to the gods, perhaps to the storyteller, "We are doomed to march them all."

On Dead American Poets and Social Networking

In Podgorica, the capital of Montenegro, I happened upon a bookstore that was called, in English, "The Last Bookstore in the World." It was also apparently one of the smallest in the world: tinier than a cobbler shop on Allenby Street in Tel Aviv, with a dozen piles of books on the floor in the language once known as Serbo-Croatian (I recognized *What We Talk About When We Talk About Love* by Carver and some Michelin guides). The owner, a withered old man wearing a tie, who sat on a stool beside his alcove and sipped raki, was used to the tourists' questions—he explained in polished English that the invasion of electronic books was also noticeable in his small country, and promised that the day was not far off when, apart from his modest establishment, there would be no more bookstores in Montenegro. (And later, because it has already been proven that the universe is expanding from sorrow, no more in the world, either.) I bought a book of poetry by a wonderful poet whose first name I cannot properly pronounce, Jovica Ivanovski, and whose language I cannot really read with my Russian, and continued on to another place I'd never been. Here I quote one of his poems that I found online in English: "I can't see the cross 'cause it's covered in thick fog, and 'cause I'm too far away." Only later did I find out that he is from a completely different country in the Balkans, Macedonia. And this is also a comment on our status: Ezra Pound had a hundred thousand followers on Twitter. Emily Dickinson was more of a Facebook person. She took privacy settings very seriously. William Carlos Williams once registered on LinkedIn. But he got nothing out of it.

On Kitsch

The reconstruction of the crime scene, which took place on the very same night as the murder, indicated that the winged creature was shot in the back of the neck as he stood relieving himself. Ten measures of wonders fell to the earth, Jerusalem received more than nine. Early in the morning the city sanitation crew washed the spatter of piss and blood from the Western Wall.

On the Oldest Jew in the World

In a letter from May 1945, from liberated Poland, my grandfather (then a young captain in the Red Army) wrote to my grandmother (then his fiancée) that he had seen an old man who was said to be the oldest Jew in the world—115 years old, maybe more. This was in the partisan camp on the banks of the Bystrica: the old man wore tattered boots that had been pulled off a German body. When my grandfather spoke to him in Yiddish the ripple of a smile appeared between his wrinkles—but he didn't answer.

Of course, he didn't have documents verifying his age. The Polish partisans said that thanks to the aura that radiated from this old gentleman, not a single one of them had fallen in battle for two years, since he had emerged from the snowy forests and joined them. (The partisans also said that in their opinion the vow of silence he had taken when his wife died ages ago—when she was only 29—was the very same trait that kept the old man alive for so long. As is known, every man is limited to a certain number of words in his lifetime, and it's not like this number is such a big prize, some of these words might also be words that you whisper in a foreign language that you don't even know, in a dream, for example, and who knows where you heard them the first time, and why is it that you repeat them night after night...)

This is what my grandfather wrote in his letter, and my future grandmother, who at that time had yet to make peace with all the quirks of her beloved, and above all with his attraction to the esoteric teachings of the East, stopped reading and put the letter in one of the crates with the books that they'd just packed in preparation for the return from the Ural Mountains to Leningrad—according to her claim, when my grandfather returned from the front she even forced him, for two months, to write her real love letters, instead of all these strange stories that he sent her from '42 onward, when he jumped onto one of the army trucks that was faltering toward Stalingrad ("It was one of those mornings when the rain poured so hard, some said that on a day like this even angels are drowning in the sky," but this is already an entirely different story...)

By the way, despite my grandfather's intense desire to believe what the Poles claimed about him, the old man actually didn't seem that old—no more than 80 or 85; his eyes were a clear and gentle shade of green. It could be that in those days, even older Jews were wandering in the forests of Europe.

More Preparations for a Long Journey

In the ashtray (and perhaps in the world) there is no more room. Icarus reaches his hand to the ceiling.

On the Brilliant Author

His last book, *Static Electricity*, also failed miserably. But then he received a six-figure advance from the tobacco companies to travel and write a guide to all the bars and cafés in the United States where smoking is still permitted. Of course, he himself smoked no more than two or three cigarettes a week, had no intention of leaving the town where he lived with his wife and two children, and from time to time, when family life allowed, he hid in his study and tried, so far with little success, to compose a short essay on the light in the stories of Anton Chekhov.

Farther than the Rain

On their third date she invited him to her apartment. When she went to the kitchen to pour the wine, he was stunned to see that in the library in her living room were the exact same books he had in his own library. To convince himself that he wasn't hallucinating, he took out one of the Calvinos and leafed through it until he came to his favorite page in the book. The bookmark left inside fell to the floor. (After a few years, when organizing all of the photographs on the computer, he thought how this was always the way with couples: in so few of the photos could the two of them be seen together. He recalled the old Indian who took their picture on the Bridge of San Luis Rey in Peru—in his trembling hand he had a broken umbrella, though it hadn't rained in many days. But there was nobody else to ask.) So as not to fall asleep and then wake up, they fucked all night.

On the Flood

Things in the plural were once called God. True, eyes were called eyes and hands were called hands, shoulders were shoulders and legs were legs. But a tree and another tree and another tree were called God. A branch and another branch and another branch were called God. A leaf and another leaf and another leaf—God. A forest, of course, was called a forest, and in the forest lived a man and a woman. Love was love, and it was easy to contain. But once, a drought began. The drought prolonged God. The man and the woman came out of the forest and delivered a prayer. But *God* did not bring God down. Another month passed. Spring began. The man and the woman found a dead bird on the ground with God moving in its belly. God, who was a leaf and another leaf and another leaf, was dead. God, who was a branch and another branch and another branch, was dying. Only up above sailed a cloud and another cloud and another cloud: God. The man and the woman wanted to count all the little Gods in which there was no rain. All the God in their palms and in the soles of their feet was not enough. Historians say that the Babylonian system of counting consisted of sixty digits. That is why to this day we divide the hours and the minutes into units of sixty. And then, suddenly, one drop of rain fell. At night the man and the woman opened their cracked mouths to the quick and heavy God that already poured without end, and folded their hands—each palm plowed with so much God—one inside the other.

Cobalt Blue

The bearded man who spontaneously combusted on Queen Helen Street in Jerusalem and burned to death was assumed to be a failed suicide bomber, but all suspicions were cast off after it turned out that (a) no explosive residue was found in the area, (b) two days before the incident he bought himself a membership to the museum, and (c) he wasn't an Arab. The passersby who saw him ignite described the flames as sky blue. The fire burst from his belly and lower back simultaneously and enveloped him instantly. He had no time to cry for help.

Prose and Poetry or the Opposite

Prose was a Persian cat. Poetry was a street cat. Or the opposite. Prose slept most of the day in the bed of the residents of his apartment and knew how to turn on the faucet. Poetry slept on the hoods of cars and knew how to open garbage bins. Or the opposite. The one time that a bird accidentally flew into the living room, Prose almost lost his mind from joy, and broke two vases trying to catch it. Poetry knew that to capture a bird one needs equal parts patience and luck. Or the opposite. Prose rarely responded when his name was called. Poetry didn't even know her name. The perils of the street shortened her life expectancy. All of the kittens she gave birth to died within a week. Prose was neutered, but sometimes masturbated on a pillow with a corner of a blanket in his mouth. He lived a long life. And so on and so forth. Or the opposite.

The Secret of Teleportation

On the back cover of his book he is pictured with his eyes shut and a cigarette in his hand; in his childhood, after he saw his father shatter a glass door with his fist in front of his mother, he began to stutter. All of the visits to the speech therapist didn't help: in the end he simply taught himself not to raise his voice. Many years later he also developed a way to smoke only in dreams, wrote a bestseller about it, and began traveling from city to city giving lectures.... He can already pack a suitcase in his sleep.

In a Distant Land

She met him a few years later, in his new country. He was happy about the children's book that she had brought for his daughter, and even read her the beginning: "When I was little like you," the big zebra said to the little zebra, "I wanted to be a zebra." "This isn't a story at all," laughed the little zebra. "Of course this is a story," said the big zebra, "this is a story about all of the things I did not want to be." After the girl fell asleep he returned to the living room. He told her that he tries to speak with the girl in Hebrew as much as he can. "I can't imagine myself without her," he said, just as he had in the café when he had told her he was considering moving to another country. His daughter was still a baby then and he had to go to her several times during the night. Sometimes he would wake her, too, and they would make love again. Each time she was again surprised to discover how little rage was stored inside him. Now she couldn't remember why she always insisted on leaving his apartment early in the morning, when even the street cats were still asleep on the hoods of cars. Tel Aviv was so gray and so beautiful when it rained. In another place their story could also begin with the words *She met him on the shortest day of winter.*

On the Black Angel

The angel that was found shot in the head in a nameless alley in Northampton was black, much blacker than the president of the United States. Even his wings were as black as a raven's nape. Only the soles of his feet were pinkish, and his girlfriend—as the tabloids discovered—was white. In the interview she gave in exchange for an undisclosed sum she said it wasn't that easy to make love with such a winged creature.

Recalculating Route

The tall old man (if he were an angel, you could also say that he was wing-heavy) sat on a park bench and read a book in Braille with his fingers. His guide dog rested at his feet. The wheel of the sun had already washed the treetops. He marked the last page he read by folding its corner.

The Number of Steps on the Moon

The launch was canceled because of a technical glitch—in those years he was convinced there would be many other opportunities. One day he discovered that he could stick his fingers inside the walls of his house, to a depth of forty centimeters or more. Since then, the retired cosmonaut would sit from time to time in the kitchen, as is customary before a long journey, hiding his palm in the wall and thinking about all the things he achieved and didn't achieve in his life.

Tiny Catalogues

This is just the beginning of a story about an amateur detective born in another country. Over the course of twenty years, since his arrival here, he collected and catalogued fingerprints from books that readers returned to the public library. Eventually he got used to the absence of twilight in Israel: I have no idea whether he expected a phone call from the police, asking for his assistance in solving one crime or another. And in general, every man needs to find the words that will end the novel he will write, even if he no longer intends to write it. (He left his own fingerprints only on the cover of a book that ended with the words, "The library of Alexandria burned all night.")

On the Art of Throwing Books

I never wrote a biography of Daniil Kharms, and to tell the truth, I also never found the link to the site that mentions one village in Ireland that holds a book-throwing competition every June, in which the winner is the one who succeeds in throwing a copy of Joyce's *Ulysses* the farthest. ("It was the rain that woke me," said Calypso to the man who promised to stay with her for the rest of his life. "How can I call this a story when I don't even know why we don't have children.")

Perfect Timing

To leave something for the family, the man who decided to commit suicide hired himself out as a one-time hit man. (He found guidance in his son's schoolbooks: a sniffling Superman and a bird with a burning tail fly toward each other at such-and-such speed: when will they meet, etc.) Day and night he made calculations to time exactly his fall from the roof with the victim's exit from the building. The only thing left to add is that certainly stories more miraculous and sad than this happen in the world. At the moment of truth he moved his watch from his right wrist to his left wrist and then dove.

Gravity

My grandmother Rosa—I've changed a few details in this story—kissed Yuri Gagarin in 1961 in an elevator in Moscow. Which is to say, this wasn't Gagarin, this wasn't in an elevator, and above all in 1961 my grandmother was already living in St. Petersburg. More than once in my childhood, I saw my grandfather floating next to her in their apartment, a few centimeters above the parquet floor. I never saw a man float higher.

Shortcuts Home

In the secondhand bookstore we found a tattered book in our language. In all the cities here it drizzles without end. The time machine technician called to say he's running late. Our lives go on.

Lunar Savings Time

This is not a political story. The couple began to keep regular sides in bed (each of them had a dozen previous partners, like the number of people who have walked on the moon). They met for the first time at a museum, beside a Monet. (He remembered that it was nighttime in the painting. She remembered that daylight had already broken, but in the sky the moon was still visible—where year zero can begin with Neil Armstrong's landing. One day could go on for almost a month.) From their pre-calendar travels they also reported a different taste in music.

The Woman Who Repaired Time Machines

Exactly like her mother, who taught her the secrets of the profession, she patches together the cracked axles of their obsolete time machines, and listens to all of their tall tales, and raises her daughter alone in the house on the hill. Maybe a day will come and she'll say to one of them— maybe the one who doesn't remember that he already recited a cummings poem to her, *maggie and milly and molly and may went down to the beach to play one day*, or maybe the one who always cuts himself more than once while shaving; or maybe to someone else, who still hasn't arrived at her time—"If time travel were possible, nobody would stay in this time."

The End of the Conflict or the Miracle of the Analog Clocks

She is from here, he is not: On the evening they fell in love only the analog clocks stood still (some irregularity in the cycle of the moon; the not-so-tasty body of Christ; the rain that falls but doesn't hurry in any language; maybe it's better that I don't try to explain how this is possible). *They can go fuck themselves*, she said, *they can go fuck themselves*, he answered. (They can go fuck themselves, the politicians, the soldiers, the terrorists, the Jews, the Muslims, the Christians, those who lower canaries into coal mines, the taxi drivers, the gamblers, the travelers in time, in ships, in helicopters, the ghosts, the settlers, those asking for the right of return, those against the right of return, the living, the dead, the demonstrators for, the demonstrators against, those who remember everything, those who forget almost nothing. To hell with them all.) This will be the end of the legend: when they got married, instead of rings, they exchanged reading glasses.

Helen's Double

To protect Helen, the Trojans found a woman who looked just like her (even in the cloudiness of her gaze) from one of the surrounding villages and brought her to Troy. Even Paris wasn't completely sure which was which (but this is already another story). Ten years later the mighty city fell (the queen of Sparta's double was finally free). On her way back to oblivion, for a brief moment, she stopped and glanced back: the art museum burned faster and fiercer than the museum of modern art.

A Piano in the Forest

This is only another story that for years I haven't managed to tell properly, but nonetheless: Like in all legends, a woman who got lost in the forest, and wandered around and could not find her way back, finally realized that she had been walking in circles for hours and started to mark the trunks of trees with lipstick. But in vain. Toward nightfall she discovered that deep in the forest stood a piano whose legs were only slightly decayed. She thought: Someone went to great effort to bring this here. To what end? Maybe I can use it to chase the wolves away. She cleaned off the leaves and branches and opened the lid and struck it with her fist and then rested her hand on the keys and waited for the darkness. She promised herself that if she found the way back, she would take piano lessons, and after a few months, when she knew how to play one composition, she would return to the forest, and search for this piano, maybe for most of her life, and finally, perhaps thanks to the signs she left on the tree trunks, she would find it and clean off the leaves and branches and open the lid... The Zen version of the legend is much shorter. And it has no piano.

On Small Betrayals

Prologue

Before the dream ended he finally found himself lying in a
dark hotel room in a different city, cold as the distance. His
insomnia gives him no peace, as sometimes happens when
he sleeps away from home. So is he sentenced, all night, to
read—there are, of course, worse nightmares than that. He
reaches his hand over the back of the woman sleeping
beside him. He gropes around for the reading lamp. A
moment before he flips the switch, he is alarmed by the
thought that she—he was suddenly confused and in his heart
he called her by his wife's name—might wake up because of
the light. And so, with the terrifying expectation that here, at
any minute, she'll find out—actually, which one of them?—that
he is reading a different book than the book he got in bed
with, he woke up.

Epilogue

After he removed from his nose the burden of the reading
glasses he'd fallen asleep wearing the night before, the
memory of the dream was erased from his consciousness.
("I dreamed something strange again last night," he said to
his wife, "but I can't remember the details." His wife glanced
briefly at the book that was lying on the dresser on her side
of the bed. She blushed a little and didn't say a word.)

And Here Is Another Legend of the King Who Loved to Rearrange His Library

Once upon a time lived a king who, at the beginning of every year, ordered that the royal library be arranged in a different way than before: by the colors of the covers, by the names of the authors, by the date of publication, by subject matter and by type, by the width of their spines, by the number of appearances of the word *time* (in the royal library there were only a few books in which the word *time* didn't appear at all), and so on and so forth. The royal mathematicians proved that the possible number of ways to arrange the library was always equal to or greater than the number of books in it. Every spring the king and his advisors reviewed the renewed beauty of the library and then went out onto the balcony and waved to the multitudes who gathered to see them and to watch the military parade. (Yes, it was spring, but it also rained slow and heavy, like in books. The snipers on the roofs searched the crowd for assassins.)

The Fine Print of Life

This is a very short history of my grandfather Arkady. His last words to my grandmother (I cannot prove that this is a true story), on the stretcher on the way to the ambulance, were, "I love you." The aperture of time closes in on him in '83, two years after he arrived in his new country. Four years earlier, in Leningrad, he took me to a market where it was possible to trade books that were forbidden to everyone for meat that was only forbidden to us. He smoked more than I smoke. He read more than I read. I remember less and less about him. His imagination was full of lions.

The Tenth Year of the Trojan War

Prologue

They say that in the tenth year of the siege of Troy, in a winter abundant in rain and love, in a twisting alleyway where if you ran too fast you'd miss the shortcut to the walls, on the second floor above the café "Baker of Tears" (this is the apartment from whose windows sometimes peeks the face of a satisfied kitten, as if they are playing cellos around the corner), hid a woman who knew the secret of flying at a medium altitude.

Epilogue

Sometimes in the night this woman took off her clothes and her underwear and clung to the ceiling like one clings to the body of a feverish, dying lover. I think of her often: I don't know with absolute certainty her name (others called her Helen). I don't know when she learned the secret of flying at low altitudes. I don't know whether, in the end, she also learned the secret of flying at significant altitudes. And in any case, I never heard a legend that tells how Menelaus's sailors saw a tiny human figure shooting over the flames consuming Troy, climbing and climbing, to the heart of the heavens. "Look," shouted one of the young men on the deck, "a flying woman!" Menelaus, weary and desperate, just shrugged. "I wish we'd never gotten into this damned war," thinks the young man after many years, when the memory of the tenth year of the siege of Troy is so blurry that any legend at all could be invented: A few years later, at the end of his wanderings, when he saw the real Helen, Menelaus was awestruck... There are many versions of this tale. All of them end similarly: From the moment of his reunion with Helen until his last day in her arms, dozens of years later, the awestruck Menelaus didn't blink, not even once.

Chromosomes

Once upon a time there was a legend about a lighthouse
that turned into a ship, and sailed all the seas of the world
and, when trying to return, was shattered on the rocks of its
childhood. Actually, I can't imagine anything more terrifying
than what happened to poet X, who woke up one morning
and discovered that he was poet Y.

If All We Have

After midnight, in a hotel in a foreign country, they turned on the radio on the nightstand (they didn't find any stations with songs that they knew). But from the balcony they could see, on the sea's surface, the wandering paintbrush of the old lighthouse, which was still in operation. *If all we have is the present, time travel is music.*

The Detective Who Falls Asleep at Crime Scenes

1

A bedroom is a metaphor for a puzzle without a clue.

2

The detective who falls asleep at crime scenes takes a second sleeping pill and pages through his notebook: A few days ago he discovered a book in this room—in the middle a page was folded at the corner. The detective makes sure that the book is still lying on the dresser beside the bed. (A little groggy, he lights a cigarette, sits down on the bed and tries to understand whose side of the bed this really is: the man's or the woman's. He lies down, tosses from side to side, sniffs the sheets—he remembers that a previous time he was deceived by the lilac fragrance of the fabric softener—and again cannot reach an unequivocal conclusion. I shouldn't have smoked here, thinks the detective, or they were so exhausted they simply fell asleep on each other's side. Embarrassed, he decides to give up this secondary mystery, quickly twisting away from the middle of the bed toward the side with the dresser and glancing at the profile of the book.) And here, exactly as he had hoped from the beginning—the page marked with a folded corner is now found at a distance of one or two chapters from the back cover. It seems to him that the greater the effect of the pill, with almost every breath, the dimmer the room's light; any minute his eyelids are going to collapse.

3

If so, thinks the detective before he falls asleep, it appears that I will decipher this mystery without leaving the room.

Superposition

Nobody really knows the people in the back pages of photo albums. But this is already another story: An aging art thief is hospitalized for three days before the operation. In the meantime, he prepares for his next caper. It's not supposed to be a complicated operation. He is about to break into two museums, in Vienna and in Munich, and from each of them steal a Klimt painting. And the doctors also promise him that after a week or two he'll be as good as new. After the fuss dies down, he'll break into the museums again and hang the paintings in each other's places. As he did with the medical records of the man in the next bed. He can still pull this off.

On Mythology

I heard this love story without an ending from an old widower, who was one of the few who survived the underground tunnels near the Dora-Mittelbau concentration camp, where the prisoners built, 30 meters beneath the earth's surface, the Nazi's V-2 rockets. In the spring of 1944, he said, a rumor spread in the tunnels that the rockets were first fired at London, but now they were capable of reaching star clusters. His opportunity came when some of the guards wandered into the deceptive zones of nights that were mornings and fell asleep. He etched a verse onto one of the rockets. This verse, he said, was not meant for God, but for a woman, whom he'd lost not far from there, in the sister camp of Dora-Mittelbau, Buchenwald. The light of day, he added, turned into myth in the Dora tunnels. But stories from there have no need for photosynthesis: "And though I walk through the valley of the shadow of death, I will fear no evil, because you, my beloved, are with me."

A Brief Note on the Heavens

In fact, the Nazi's opposition to Expressionism had a marginal effect on Emil Nolde. Sure, his paintings were removed from the walls of the Reich's museums, but nobody knew what to do with the porcelain heavens decorated with tulips that he'd painted. (Of course, measures were taken: In 1941 Emil Nolde was forbidden to paint new paintings. After failing to thwart the evil decree, Emil Nolde began to paint in secret. He called the series of small watercolors he painted in those years by the paradoxical name "Unpainted Pictures.") Even the cracks that spread from the edges to the center made the heavens look like an old painting.

Heidegger's Soul

Winter is a city, and in this city Martin Heidegger is dreaming something like this: An old gypsy woman is harassing him on the street, next to a house with an even-numbered address. And yes, she wants to ask him a riddle. In Heidegger's dream he walks out of an office-supply store with a conical paperweight while the old woman is dragging a sack of something swaying back and forth and perhaps breathing—in his heart Heidegger guesses correctly: these aren't books. The old woman asks Heidegger if she should wait while he nears a solution. Heidegger, who is uncomfortable being seen in such company in public, and is dumbfounded that anyone let her wander around like this in the middle of the city, hurriedly points with the cone in his hands to a torn piece of cloud being dragged on the edge of a fleet of broad clouds in the sky. He declares that this torn piece of cloud, this and no other, is his soul. The old gypsy shrugs and says that this is not the riddle. She rests the sack on the sidewalk and rummages inside. Heidegger wakes covered in sweat. From every direction air raid sirens wail.

Hannah

The privilege between therapist and patient is not the same, of course, as the clear one-way relationship (outwardly) between an author and a character. But I must honor the profession of A., and keep the name he gave her, Hannah. Even when he begins to describe their first meeting, he admits that he himself entertains the idea of adding some small, harmless inventions to these events. Smoking, for example: she was pleased when he told her it wouldn't bother him if she lit a cigarette. "If time travel is possible," he said. "we'd always be meeting time travelers."

"You're quoting Stephen Hawking," she said, "I know who that is." She asked in embarrassment if she should lie on the couch. "So there are still movies in the distant future," he remarked with a smile, and said that it didn't matter to him. Hannah remained seated. Her face was pleasant, a bit long; her brown hair was pulled back with a barrette.

"Everyone is hiding something," she said quietly, "I could have escaped to any time I wanted. But I chose to come here, to this time. To you." She had a slight accent, he wasn't able to identify its origin.

"Let's say that I accept what you are claiming," A. countered. "But why me?"

"Because I read about my test case in your book," she replied and rested her gaze on the books to the right of the door—from one of the shelves jutted a stack of record albums he'd found a few years ago, when he was cleaning out his parents' house—"a book you haven't written yet."

"When will I write it?" He rose from his chair and walked to the curtained window. He remembered that when he went out to meet her in the waiting room she'd quickly removed her sunglasses. He noticed a thin scar above her right eyebrow.

"In four years," she answered. "You will treat me for two years and then I'll return home."

"If you've already read all of this," he said, returning to his desk, "If you know how I'll treat you…" He inserted a cassette into a tape recorder and pushed the record button, "then tell me how I shall begin."

She puffed on her cigarette and was quiet for a moment, and then said, "From the beginning. I was born in 2303. My parents had a house outside the city. At the age of eight…" Hannah came back every week, exactly at the agreed-upon hour, for two years. In the winter of 2004 she called him the day before her appointment and said that she was going away for a few months.

These days A. is writing a book on his treatment method. He tells me that the writing is progressing nicely, but he's gotten to the chapter about the case of the woman who claimed that her grief was from the future, and now he has total writer's block. He even blames his writing problems on his insufficient knowledge of modern physics.

"Did you know that this isn't such an outlandish idea, time travel," he points out, "Even according to Einstein, if we travel close to the speed of light it's possible to get to the future. And there are other serious physicists who have proposed models for time machines with which it would be possible to reach the past." On the Internet he read about a machine proposed by the mathematician Kurt Gödel: Its unique quality is that it can indeed allow returning to the past, but only to a time later than the moment when it is assembled.

"I didn't understand the equations," he says, "but it's clear that because the window of time you can travel to is limited here, Hannah must have used a different method. Unless someone already built this time machine several years ago, but hasn't told us." All of this has made him think about theory in a field a bit closer to his own. Even if time travel were possible, he claims, travelers from the future would dream here only dreams that they already dreamed in the original time from which they came. Perhaps the soul cannot travel so far. Of course, he admits that this is not truly connected to his treatment of Hannah.

I suggest that he simply set aside this chapter for the time being and in the meantime continue writing the rest of the book. But A. says that he promised his publisher he'd turn in the manuscript at the end of November; it's September already, and the holidays are coming—the time of year when patients from the past tend to come back. So he is flooded with work. It seems he'll have to give up on her story.

On Cain and Abel

On the pedestrian mall, in the display window of a secondhand store, he saw a Remington that appeared to be brand new. The last man on earth smashed the window and dragged the machine all the way back to the fourth floor of the five-star hotel where he lived. As soon as he was beset by his usual writer's block, he hurled it from the window. Once a year he visited the lemon tree beside which he had buried his only reader, the second-to-last man on earth.

On Art History

...And in those days the king imprisoned all of the painters in his kingdom and sentenced them to life in the highest-security prison in the kingdom. (One poet, who was imprisoned with the painters after publishing a poem called "I Am Not a Poet," wrote in a letter that was smuggled out of the prison: "The fourth dimension is nothing but light... thus even time is not lacking here—so you can get used to even the scantest light in the cell." Several decades later the king died—naturally, the painters also died. So in the next generation there were no painters in the kingdom.) Of course, the king's son, who was a reformer, ordered that the prison be turned into a museum.

On the Writers' Conference

The writer from the moon has a British accent. He reads from a novella set in India. Every time he pronounces the word elephant, the refined audience blushes with pleasure. After him, a Brazilian writer lectures on "The Nightlife of the Short Story." In a plaza outside the auditorium, a young woman plump from love is smoking the last cigarette of the evening. In moment she will throw the butt into the sky.

The Little Ballad of the Writing Ghost

Of all the ghosts I've heard about, my favorite is one that lives in one of the castles in northern Scotland, a castle that has been a hotel for decades. The ghost is revealed early in the morning, when it sits hunched over a table in the dining room (except for a few days in the summer, when the room is flooded with light from the wide windows carved out of the ceiling) and writes in ballpoint pen in a wide-ruled notebook. Over the years the ghost has developed a complete immunity to the different background noises, and not even the frequent conversations between strangers about some used bookstore they've discovered in one of the villages in the area (on one of the piles of books there, reaching as high as the moon, sleeps a black cat; and wouldn't you know, hiding in the pile is also a first edition of T.S. Eliot) distract it from its labor for even a moment.

Apart from the chair that it occupies in the dining room, the writing ghost tends not to bother the guests, for example, by changing the home pages on laptop computers, or smashing windows with the skillful flinging of record albums (which are obtained for an exorbitant sum from the secondhand record store, attached to the used bookstore, which are jointly owned, though without a typical presence of pets), or even just switching the reading glasses of the couples who leave them on the dressers beside the bed. And it will never be heard weeping. One of the legends says that it is the ghost of an author who was once a guest in the hotel. And that he will stay there until he finishes his second novel.

On the Logic of Legends

There was a legend about a man in an electric wheelchair, who traveled every morning on the shoulder of the highway, and always stopped at the same roadside restaurant. There was, for example, a legend about a young woman named Clytie, who fell in love with the god of the sun. While he was charging the wheelchair's battery, he told his regular waitress a story from Greek mythology. But the god did not take heed of her love and she turned into a sunflower. After the battery was charged, he would head home. That way she could always watch him on his journey through the sky.

Three Moons

1

And of all the conspiracy theories my favorite is the one that claims man never landed on the moon (and that the pictures were staged by NASA and the US government). A similar charge, by the way, appears in the letters of the opponents of Amerigo Vespucci, which more than once warned the king of Portugal that his sailor was nothing more than a syphilitic pirate who discovered new lands with the same frequency with which he scratched his balls. And of all the versions of conspiracy theories about the faking of the moon landing, my favorite is the one that claims that it's impossible to land on the moon for the simple reason that there is, in fact, no moon. In the Soviet Union they also knew this well, but they could not expose the American fraud, because nobody knew how the Soviet people would react to this news: this could destroy socialism in an instant. Sometimes this is all we have in common, all human beings, a pretty picture in the night sky.

2

"If you don't believe me, Google it,"—what kind of beginning is this for a true story? In any case, every year the moon and the Earth grow approximately three centimeters farther apart. And what kind of ending is this? "There are people in the world who cut themselves to feel that there is something true in all of this."

3

Dante's shadow had green eyes. Together they went out to observe the stars. And Scheherazade tells all of her magic in bed. A white sail—a sign of the horizon. A black sail—a funny dream. And only my great-grandfather, what nerve he had! All his life he shaved his head completely (and only at the end of his life, when he'd already been sent to the nursing home, did his hair grow back savagely. He actually held on like that year after year after year. The nurse who tried to comb it complained to me that he always invented impossible stories for her: How in '43 in Stalingrad, he killed five snipers with a non-standard slingshot, while my great-grandmother was sitting in the Urals weaving threads of moonlight into sails for Russian jets... How in his childhood in Voronitch, he was afraid to eat ice cream. The women in his family—his aunt, for example, as pretty as a music box dancer, or his mother, as elegant as a birch tree—tried to convince him to wait for the ice cream in the spoon to melt a little. He didn't see the logic. What is colder: ice cream, or the weather in a city whose palaces aren't sinking because the ice in the ground isn't melting? So many things have changed since then: The northern lights can already be seen in the countries of the Maghrib. On a Greek island, they found Venus once again, this time with her arms. My great-grandfather used to leap to his feet and wave his hands and laugh and remember. The nurse would tell him to go on with his story and in the meantime let her comb his hair, and then my great-grandfather would relax for a moment and sit and murmur, *Yes indeed, the words of old men make the world spin.* And then he'd grow enraged and shout: *It never was and never existed! My curls make the world spin.*)

Half-life

These days the length of the lives of clouds is equal to the lifespan of man. Aegeus goes to sleep in the room that was his son's. Far from there, in the great labyrinth of Crete, the minotaur also has nowhere to escape.

An Innocent Legend

Once upon a time there was a man who always dreamed intoxicating dreams about flying at a medium altitude. He feared that the day would come when he would not be able to resist the temptation to continue his flight right out the window. He began to sleep with a five-kilo weight tied to each leg. "If this is your only eccentricity," said a woman who'd fallen in love with him, "I don't really care. Maybe once you could even infect me with your flying dreams. And then we could tie our legs together." And the storyteller added, "And this is the whole plot, believe it or not. They lived happily ever after, to this very day."

Braver

And this superhero disguised himself as a graphomaniac. Once a month he sent a new book to all the publishing houses and went out to save the world from annihilation. More than once he woke up from a nightmare in which one of his manuscripts is accepted.

Stepping in the Same River Twice

The plumber who was called to the Museum of Modern Art at midnight was not especially interested in modern art (and particularly not at midnight). He brought with him a strange machine, a kind of mechanical metal snake that made more noise than a classroom of children in front of a Mapplethorpe photograph. "This machine can open a clog even in a garage," he said to the museum director (who was already imagining the sweet scandal of galleries flooded with shit, and hoped in his heart that the master craftsman would fail). After he finished his work with unquestionable success, he said, in the manner of all reactionary plumbers, "You need to hang whoever designed your sewage system. There isn't a single normal pipe here."

More Experiments in Quantum Mechanics
A story for two

Let's assume that on the other side of the wall stands a woman with whom you are about to fall in love. Let's assume that on the other side of the wall stands a man with whom you are about to fall in love. Let's leave out for a moment the probability of a piano passing through a wall, because it's not the constant of love that we are trying to discover here, nor the two identical fingerprints, nor the two identical snowflakes, and not even the two cranes who were scheduled on the same morning on the same street to lift two pianos to two different apartments in the same building and so on—now, let's assume that there is no wall.

Fiction

And the last man in the world is writing a novel.

A More Innocent Legend

This will be the legend: One god fell in love with one woman, whose hair grew so long that one night she cut off her braid and used it to lower herself from a high castle. To confuse her enemies, the god began to blow and extinguish the stars in the world's skies. Of every star he blew out he asked: She loves me, she loves me not, she loves me, she loves me not... A bit before sunrise, when he realized that he would find neither an answer nor relief in the endless fields of stars, he gave up and hid his face in the moon. And the storyteller commented: "The love lives of the gods, like those of humans, aren't simple. Thus were the seas and craters on the moon created."

The Labyrinth of Sleep

This page and a half also remained deliberately empty of any story. In a bookstore on Diagonal Street in Barcelona, whose sign hanging out front described exactly what was preserved within, "Rare Used Books," I saw volumes of *The Thousand and One Nights*, printed in Braille in Spanish. The store owner (an old dandy with a colorful silk scarf wrapped around his throat who leaned on a walking stick) justified the scandalous prices of these white books with the claim that among their previous owners was none other than Jorge Luis Borges—who had even copied a story from one of the volumes, which had never appeared in any other version of *The Thousand and One Nights*.

Some time ago the story was translated into Hebrew with the title "The Labyrinth of Sleep." A summary of the story, more or less, goes like this: One of the kings of Babel dreams that his young son dies. The king sinks (in another dream) into despair and stops looking after the interests of the kingdom. An advisor who arrives from a distant province suggests that the king sleep one night in his son's small bed. "Your son's spirit is tormenting you," says the advisor. "You must explain to it that it has no place in this world."

In his dream the king does just that. He falls asleep in his son's bed and dreams that he wakes up in his own bed, and discovers that his son is lying next to him, lifeless. He reaches for his sword. He wakes up horrified in his son's bed; then he wakes up again, in his own bed. His sword is smeared with blood. (In an alternative version of this tale, writes Borges, the son is murdered by enemies and his body placed in his father's bed.)

At the end of the story Borges remarks, "Some years ago I encountered, in a used bookstore not far from the Mexico Library, a copy of *The Thousand and One Nights*; to read it I had to learn writing I had been sentenced to know since my birth. I could not afford the asking price; when he noticed my distress, the seller proposed that I borrow one of the volumes of the book, in exchange for a symbolic deposit: My pocket watch. I returned to my apartment with the third volume (out of five) and after a few nights I brought it back to the store, unable to find within it the six hundred and second night of the tale: the night that Scheherazade tells a story that is the opening frame of all the thousand and one nights, about a sultan who slept with a new virgin every night and in the morning cut off her head, until Scheherazade arrived and began to tell him stories for a thousand and one nights, including the story with no way out: the six hundred and second night.... But it wasn't all in vain. While my fingers were tentatively exploring the book, I discovered in the margins of one of the hundreds of glittering pages a different ending to this tale about the king from Babel, grieving in his dream." The king wakes up in his bed from a dream that happens inside a dream and sees that his sword has been placed in its scabbard, like a bookmark. His seven-year-old son is asleep at his side, unharmed. The boy wakes up and says, "I'm sorry, Father. I was afraid to sleep alone."

Aeneas, the Runner
(and Three Other Small Paradoxes)

1

The legend tells that Mary Magdalene arrived at the feet of Christ with a rose in one hand; with her other hand she hid the petals—"If you can guess exactly how many petals this rose has," she said, "I will take you down from the cross." Jesus answered immediately, "An infinity."

2

In the Infinity Hotel (some called it the Tower of Babel) were an infinite number of rooms, and always an infinite number of guests in them. Every time a new guest arrived, the guest in room 101 would be asked to move to room 102, the guest in room 102 would be asked to move to room 103, the guest in room 103 would be asked to move to room 104, and so on. The guest at the end of the hall would be asked to move up one floor. The guest in room 201... and so on. Some days one of the elevators didn't work. The windows on the twentieth floor were shattered by lost birds and on the floors too high to count, from frost. The nighttime concierge spoke broken English, and couldn't explain to the anonymous caller that the guest registered under the name Norma Jean had already checked out.

3

Zeno, the philosopher, confused everyone with the paradox about Achilles and the tortoise: Achilles is placed at some distance behind the tortoise. Achilles will advance at double the speed of the tortoise, but will not catch up with it. At first he will cover half the distance that separates him from the tortoise. And then another half of the distance. And so on... Maybe Zeno meant not the actual distance, but the distance in memory.

4

Many legends tell us that Aeneas, escaping from the defeated Troy, takes his old father on his back. On this strange journey they take turns sleeping—the father most often, while grasping the neck of his son, whose strength begins to wane over time. The father's dreams are beautiful: he dreams about rivers that twist by almost ninety degrees to the heavens. And in these rivers float enormous stone statues of heroes, statues that once stood in the plazas of Troy.

The son, on the other hand, falls asleep for short periods, like the blinking of a predator. Every time the anguished old man wakes him up and pleads: "Leave me here, Aeneas. Leave me, I'm begging you... If you continue alone, you will make much faster progress. In any case my days are numbered." The son refuses. In his heart he curses his father for not letting him rest and get the sleep he needs.

This journey goes on for many days and many nights. Eventually the father asks a final time. "Oh, my glorious son, in the name of Zeus almighty, in the name of all that gods that ever were and ever will be, I beg you, leave me here." And then Aeneas awakens from the dream in which he is dragging his father on his back until the end of time.

And even all of this was in vain. The father dies suddenly. Aeneas tries to cheer himself: My father's heart, he says to himself, beats at the exact pace that my heart beats. Therefore I no longer feel his heartbeats. Our hearts were one... The old father, in his dream, closes his hand over his son's chest, interlocks his fingers, and holds on with all his strength.

Aeneas stops for a moment. He takes a deep breath and breaks into a wild run.

The father, who no longer speaks, doesn't let go.

Aeneas, who suddenly can no longer fall asleep as he runs, is already faster than a panther's shadow.

thank you

833

316-717

On the Old Man Who Thought He Was Don Quixote

He is a regular customer at this café, where smoking is still allowed (where we all sit and cough). His limbs are thin and emaciated, his yellowish cheeks adorned with a matching fuzz; his eyes a depressed shade of green. It seems to me that I have already written a similar story: For years he's been breaking into apartments whose owners have traveled abroad for a few days, to rearrange the books in the guest room (mostly according to the year the book was published, from the oldest book on the highest shelf on the right, to the newest book on the lowest shelf on the left). He fought in three of Israel's wars, and in general his life is abundant with so many adventures he cannot forget that it would not be an exaggeration to say that he lived twice, even more.

The Second Mark of Cain

All his life he wanders restlessly in the world, protected by a mark the Bible does not deliver, with not even a hint (one legend tells of a waterfall of roads that washed away his anger; even the whores loved his tenderness; on every cup he drank from, upon each back he caressed, in all the books he opened, he left a fingerprint).

Untitled. Another Angel

The angel who fell in the heavy rain of 2003 remained in a coma for six years. In the seventh year he woke up and asked for a cigarette. He didn't remember his name or his assignment on earth, but knew how to play chess expertly. Something about the snow globe with the Eiffel Tower inside that one of the nurses put on the shelf beside his bed frightened him. In a sudden rage he smashed it against the wall. Later he apologized. His wings atrophied from lack of use. The doctors weren't convinced that he could ever fly again. Not one muscle in his bearded face moved when they brought up the idea of amputation.

Lie to Me, Muse

All of the creases in the maps were flattened long ago. On this journey not ten years pass, but a whole life. Even the old man resting on the bench damp from rain cannot recognize his son from a picture in a wallet.

Penultimate Rain

You've obviously heard the story about the man who suffered from a terminal illness and suddenly got well, and the doctors had no idea what caused this. He tried to recall what medication he'd stopped taking, or which prayers he'd begun to skip. He tried to reconstruct everything he'd said to his wife, and what he wanted to say to her and didn't dare. He was so afraid that the illness would return that he once dreamed that all night it rained and if the rain ceased before morning, he would die. (Coleridge wrote—in rather different wording—a legend about a man who dreams that he is walking barefoot on a road paved with shattered glass. When he wakes up he discovers that only one of his feet is bleeding.) On the same night it did indeed rain, harder than any story.

Theory of Relativity

In the table of contents this story comes before its predecessor. The students asked the Zen master: "Can you tie your shoes with one hand?" He answered: "If I'm in a real hurry."

The Woman Who Waited for the Volcano

I don't remember whether in Greek mythology, the best collection of true stories that I know, there is indeed a story about a woman who heard a prophecy that she would meet her true love on the bank of the river of fire. She sailed to an island abandoned for eons by its residents, where, as was told in legends, there was a volcano that hadn't erupted in so many years that some suggested returning to settle the island as in earlier days... Others warned that the ground at the foot of the volcano was still not completely healed. In any event: In the prophecy it was said that she would have to wait for half of her life, until the volcano awakened. Her brother, a lame blacksmith, outfitted her with armor to withstand the heart of the lava flow. She studied the behavior of the birds.

The Old Man Who Invented the Time Machine

He has some naïve paintings that his father painted, which are more precious to him than all the books on physics and mathematics that disappointed him many times in the past. I don't think this story will be about these paintings. His sons didn't get along here and returned to St. Petersburg; coincidentally or not, the name of his granddaughter, Alex, is identical to my name... according to the photos she is taller than her mother by a head. She is studying, he told me proudly, pharmaceutical science at a university in Moscow. A few months ago, when he was ill—a mild flu, but of course at his age it's advisable to be wary of complications—he asked if I would check his mailbox; perhaps she had sent him a letter.

When he found out that apart from his electric bill I threw away all of the junk mail that was crowding his mailbox—takeout menus from neighborhood restaurants, mostly—he smiled slightly and quickly hid his disappointment; then he admitted, with a much wider smile, that sometimes he keeps a few of these flyers.

In Russia, so he told me, he worked in a classified military facility; but in the nineties, like so many others, he didn't have trouble getting an emigration visa: he'd already retired in the mid-eighties. And so he completed his independent research on time travel later, in Israel. His major discovery—if I understood correctly—is that time is compressed and chaotic in equal measure. To go back—the future, he said, never interested him—one must be accurate to the last detail.

When he told me about his work he admitted that for my sake he simplified everything down to a "popular" level. "For example," he said after I told him that I was a writer— "imagine that one night you dream that you've been given the chance to change one word in one sonnet that was written at the end of the thirteenth century. It would be impossible to know exactly how many people had already read this sonnet in the six hundred or so years that have passed since then, how it has already influenced their lives, or—and this complicates the matter more—didn't influence them at all... this is inconceivably complicated, and this is only a sonnet, and a single word, or a single image, and don't forget, only a dream...

"And now try to imagine a boy of six or seven, maybe in Marseilles, in the fifteenth century, chasing a butterfly... will he catch it? You undoubtedly say, what's the difference, there are a billion butterflies like this one, but how can we know whether a flutter of this butterfly's wings won't in the end set off a storm in the middle of the Atlantic Ocean, where at the time three caravels are sailing from a small port in Andalusia, on their way to India, and they would have to turn westward, to the new India..."

These days the old inventor of the time machine lives in a small apartment on a leafy street in Tel Aviv. With his pension he buys a few fruits and vegetables, and sends them to the year 1942, to a Leningrad under siege, to a young, dark-eyed woman who will one day be his wife.

On the Painter of Doors

And so this painter used to go into residential buildings, jam a match into the light switch in the hall, drag his easel up the stairwell in search of another door he would paint, and so on. (Sometimes he would stay and work in the stairwell in the classic silence of night.) He painted, in oil on canvas, more than three hundred doors. It's not unreasonable to assume that all his life he has loved the same woman.

Two More Zen Masters

One Zen master showed another Zen master how he walked through the air, from one bank of a flowing river to the other (and immediately returned out of breath). He explained, "The river is the void that separates the two sides of another, hidden river." The second Zen master clapped his hands at the trick and then (many years later, when the rivers had become polluted and on the riverbanks grew bridges and a promenade and skyscrapers) showed his colleague how he points his index finger at the nose of a stray cat, and after hesitating for a few moments it sniffs the finger in curiosity.

Untitled, Etc: A Copy Without an Original

It appears that I won't try to expand this little story about a simulacrum into a complete thriller—I admit that I again don't have the courage or even the despair felt by someone about to rob a bank, or, in my case, begin to write a novel. And so it was: In the morning the blinking computer screen connected to the biometric database announced the error "invalid match." At four-thirty in the afternoon the young computer expert dispatched to the district arrived at the police station: tall and bony, with a square haircut and transparent complexion, almost unhealthy. He explained that the database contained dozens of artificial fingerprints, which were created by an image-processing program, in a lab. "We use these prints to test the integrity of the algorithm. But this only happens in a simulation, like when we test a new version... and not in an operational situation, like you're running. Ah, smoking is permitted here?" he asked with delight when he saw two uniformed policemen enter the room with cigarettes in hand. "The reason for the error message," he declared, "is that the program identified a perfect match between the fingerprint that you found and one of the fabricated prints." He lit a cigarette. "So what can we do?" asked the detectives. "As always," he replied, "Restart the computer and try again. But if the error message returns, maybe this is indeed the criminal you are looking for."

The Loop of Orpheus

An ancient legend tells that Orpheus went down to the underworld twice, and the second time he also did not manage to meet Hades' terms. Because even then there were no new stories to tell. And perhaps there were no stories at all. (When he left the underworld it was night. His knees betrayed him. Before he collapsed he saw that the moon in the sky was twice its normal size, or more. He thought this was because of his music. Everything else was lost.) Another legend, from a bit later, tells that the second time Orpheus could not fail: Before he and Eurydice began to ascend to the ground, he gouged out his own eyes.

Another Lullaby

A summary of the previous chapters: As in legends—or soap operas—the brother and sister were separated at birth, delivered to two adoptive families, met by chance many years later after missing two different connections at the hell that some call Heathrow, fell in love, moved in together, got married, etc. They are the most beautiful couple imaginable. (In another nocturnal story, an angel with lips cracked like the earth after a drought would whisper in their dream that they shouldn't get pregnant. On his way out, so as to be sure that they wouldn't forget his warning, he would knock the lamp off of the table and they would wake, and clean up the pieces and wonder what exactly had happened, and why the alarm wasn't working.) Maybe snowflakes are the real blood of the world.

On Accuracy

In the poet's library there were volumes whose pages gave off a light scent of jasmine. The upstairs neighbor, who came in once to return the poet's lost mail, was surprised by the vast number of ashtrays filled with cigarette butts lining the windowsills of the apartment. "So... writing a lot?" he asked, and the poet corrected him, "Smoking a lot."

On the Metamorphosis

Once upon a time there was a tree who, of all the trees in the forest, fell in love all the way to his roots with a woman who passed through the forest. The metamorphosis was his only escape: he had to turn into a man and go out into the world to find her. (He was stabbed during a fight in a port city in the east. When he started to bleed he could no longer feel his legs. He didn't die. He boarded a ship that was lost in the Straits of Gibraltar. When he drowned he found a remedy in the intoxication of the depths. He didn't die. In one of the versions of this legend, which ends after many years of wandering and hardship, the tree returns to the forest of his birth, where he hangs himself.) He could not forget her, even when the wind blew.

Super Zen

Like many superheroes, in her everyday life she works at a dreary job: as a clerk at the post office. But from time to time she has to use her special powers even from behind the counter. Once a thief entered her post office and pointed the gun in his trembling hand at her. She said, *The Buddha's heart was also not on the right side.* Enlightenment was within reach.

The Story as Another Perfect Crime

His motive remained a mystery. At his sentencing he refused to express remorse, and even the series of character witnesses assembled by his defense attorney couldn't sweeten the judgment decreed on the author: life imprisonment. Nevertheless, in light of his good behavior in prison, no more than a year had passed and the warden permitted him to keep a computer and a printer in his cell. (The other prisoners used his services to write letters to lovers and to the president.)

Motive from the Past

Prologue

In the autumn of 1941 another volcano erupts on the island of Sumatra while German newspapers are rarely reporting on a serial killer who is terrorizing the city of Berlin; it may be that the censors are asking to conceal the existence of such an antihero in the capitol of the Third Reich; but perhaps this also has something to do with legitimate editorial concerns; indeed these days the progress of the war in the east is making dizzying headway. In the *Berliner Morgenpost* (one of the widely distributed newspapers), for example, we find only two news items; the first, from the 23rd of September, tells that the serial killer shot his victims with a sniper's rifle while they rode bicycles on the Boulevard Unter den Linden. The public is asked to be on alert; the second item, from the middle of October, reports on—as a matter of fact, after a two-week delay—the arrest of the shooter; few details are being released: a detective in charge of the investigation is quoted as saying that a failed romance was uncovered between the murderer and the third of the nine victims, a young woman with pale eyes named Margareta. (An unfulfilled passion—a clichéd motive, if not banal. But to hide his motive from the police, and maybe even from himself, the diabolical logic of the murderer led him to commit, in the month of September alone, eight more random killings.)

Epilogue

The end of the item mentions that the murderer was sentenced, and sent to death row at the Plattensee prison.

Lamentation

And the king from the East shall conquer their land, and cut out the right eye of every man. Because their land is harder than a diamond. And the king from the West shall defeat the king from the East and conquer their land and cut out the left eye of every woman. Because their rivers are the color of topaz. Or the opposite: The women's right eyes, the men's left eyes. Because symmetry is only a knitting needle in the skein of beauty. And one woman shall say to one man, "Birds fly in an arrow formation to shield themselves from the wind." And he shall say, "But there are only two of us." In the air no signs shall remain of the desperate beating of our wings.

The Essence of Art. The Essence of Night

And one art collector bequeathed his entire collection of paintings to the airport. The first exhibition opened in the departure terminal. (Nor will the digital version of this story have a pause button.) Something completely different happened to a Zen monk, whom passersby saw sitting in the high branches of a lemon tree. To their amazement the monk replied that he climbed the tree because of a tiger. "We don't see a tiger here," the passersby said with surprise. "So climb up here too," he said.

True Legends

The piano tuner claimed that he went blind at the age of six, from a genetic illness. In his childhood, he added, he heard a legend from his mother about the one and only piano in the world that, if he tuned it, would restore his vision. (We guided him to our old Czech piano. After a while he suddenly stopped tinkering inside the instrument and stood up. With the tuning fork in his hand, he tried to reach the palace made of spider webs above the window frame.) What a sad story, we said to ourselves: Undoubtedly he will then have to wander the world until he finds and tunes the one and only piano that will make him blind again.

The Author and His Wife

Prologue

On the first evening after his wife had gone to visit her sister in the north, the author discovered that one of the drawers in their bedroom dresser was locked. He couldn't find a key for the drawer anywhere. A suspicion arose in his heart that his wife was writing a book, and that she was hiding it from him. This idea that his wife was writing—in truth, that she wrote better than he did—gnawed at the author. That same night, when he lay troubled in their partly empty bed and couldn't fall asleep, he decided to break into the dresser: if indeed he found a manuscript there (a novel, undoubtedly!), he would steal it and publish it himself. He jumped out of bed, turned on every light in the house, took out—to be completely honest, for the first time—a screwdriver from the toolbox he'd received for his birthday and set to work. After three hours of chiseling and digging and scratching, exhausted but satisfied, he examined the contents of the drawer.

The Author's Note

When writing a detective novel the author who doesn't know how to keep the plot going has two lifelines at his disposal: the first is a dream in which the detective discovers the metaphorical meaning of the same mystery that he wants to solve; the second is a ringing telephone, waking the detective from the dream in which he was about to receive a hint to the solution of the mystery. Since this simple tale is far from being a novel, let alone a detective novel, I almost don't need to point out that at the time I wrote it, I didn't have to use one of the aforementioned techniques. (Indeed, after breaking into the drawer it became clear to the author that he suspected his wife for nothing: there was only a compass, waterproof matches, a folded map of the French port city of Marseilles, etc.)

Epilogue

In the days afterward the author focused his melancholy thoughts on the love story he had promised to write for his wife before she left. From time to time he opened and closed folders on the computer, looking for an old story that might be fitting, or another twist.

And Love and Modern Art and Other Wondrous Stories

Once upon a time a young couple kissed for at least ten minutes in a sculpture garden, and didn't cease their labors even when the alarm went off, exactly at the moment when the janitor began erasing the painting that was painted by an unknown artist in lipstick on the restroom mirror in the museum. And once upon a time a Chinese emperor ordered all the books in China to be burned. (Where there is also a volcano that, from time to time, you can hear singing.)

Franz Kafka, the Lost Years

A Draft of an Impossible Novel

In May 1924 Kafka is on his deathbed, but in June, as if he were some character in a story he never wrote, his condition improves. One month and then another go by and then, in August, for the first time, he even travels alone on the streets of Prague and for a few minutes gets lost. Brod unwillingly returns his letters and Kafka burns them on the banks of the Vltava, "On a night submerged in stars." After two years, he and Dora are married. They often speak of traveling to America, but then Dora becomes pregnant, and they postpone their plans until after the birth, and then until after their daughter starts kindergarten, then school, and so on and so forth. (In 1935, after many pleas from his wife, Kafka goes to his father's grave. While standing there he is surprised by the brightness of the sky, "almost like a blank page.") In 1937, in the winter, their daughter falls ill. In the spring—which again came early that year—she recovers from pneumonia, but on the advice of the doctors she is forbidden from traveling. Kafka is dismissed from his job at an insurance agency in 1939. In 1941 the three of them are sent to Theresienstadt. "If I had to imagine this place, if I had to write about it before I knew it existed"—admits Kafka during their first days in the concentration camp, to a man who claimed to have read *The Castle*—"I would have imagined it all differently." One of the small consolations he notes to himself is the weather report of one of the camp newspapers, which, every day, accurately predicts most of the expected weather in Theresienstadt, and also in London, Tokyo, and New York. As though life has not been reduced to a single point on a map. In the winter of 1943, their daughter dies from a second case of pneumonia and malnutrition. One night in 1944 Dora takes him by the hand and says that they must travel to America, it cannot be put off any longer. The next day, when the Red Cross arrives at the Nazis' showcase camp, she hangs herself. In September Kafka is sent to Auschwitz. There, too, he survives by way of a miracle—"Because there was no other way." A year and a half after the liberation of the camp he sails to Palestine. He is sixty-three years old, his health again weak, his Hebrew very flawed. He has an easier time with Yiddish, but this doesn't receive a warm welcome. His struggle to adjust is no different than that of other Holocaust survivors: after two years his situation stabilizes. He Hebraizes his name to Ephraim Kaspi, finds a part-time job at Bank Mizrahi that doesn't demand much contact with the public, though barely getting by he still insists on not writing down his nightmares, about "dogs barking on the platform in a foreign language." He works for several years and then lives on the reparations from Germany. One rainy November Max Brod suddenly appears in Israel. While expressing surprise that a native of Prague has chosen to live in Tel Aviv (on Gideon Street, in a house where the poet David Avidan will someday live) and not in Haifa or Jerusalem, he tells Kafka offhandedly that he kept hidden some of his stories. "My name is Ephraim now," answers the aging Kafka. Brod asserts that the time has come to publish the stories. He offers many arguments, and even tells Kafka that at some universities (in Europe, and especially in Berlin) there is new interest in the work that he published in his time. Kafka turns a deaf ear. At their last meeting, in a café crowded with theatergoers coming from a production at Habima, Brod shouts in German, "You ungrateful bastard. It's too bad that the Nazis didn't kill you." Afterward he apologizes, but doesn't return the stories. Kaspi goes home, tears a map out of a telephone book he has no use for, and tries to plan a walk that will in the end get him lost in the middle of Tel Aviv, even for just a few minutes. From then on he refuses to open Brod's letters because he is afraid that he will discover that Brod is marketing his work in Germany. So we have no explanation why, in a moment of weakness, Kafka-Kaspi nevertheless sends the journal *Keshet* a semi-autobiographical story that he wrote in Hebrew. The story, called "The Man Who Dreamed Twice," arrived in 1963, typewritten with handwritten corrections as if by an elementary-school student. Its publication was delayed from issue to issue, until in the end it was forgotten. (Some of the quotations above were quoted to me from memory by A. A., the editor of the journal at the time.) In the closing scene of the story the narrator returns, after many years, to the city of his birth, Prague, accompanied by his daughters. They walk to the house where he used to live. He knocks on the door of the old apartment. The young woman who owns the house comes outside, closing the door so that the cats won't get out. She asks with surprise who the old gentleman is, and the women with him. (Because of the cameras she guesses that they are tourists.) She tries to rephrase the question in English, but he has already answered, for the first time in many years, "Kafka." He pauses briefly, as if he is not completely convinced that this is how things unfold, but then he smiles in acceptance, and adds, in Czech, "Franz Kafka. And these are my daughters, Iris, Milena, and Tali. I once lived here, too." This strange optimism is Kaspi's lot in the last years of his life. He often goes to the beach and to the cinema, buys a camera and a record player and, fittingly, takes many pictures of the sea and in the evenings listens to Bach, and with great pleasure reads Agnon. Two weeks after the Six-Day War the elderly Kafka joins a neighbor whose son has returned safely from the battlefield on a trip to the Western Wall. "This was my first time in Jerusalem," says Kaspi on the way home, "It is truly more beautiful than a postcard." One night in the autumn of 1967 he begins to cough and spit up blood. He fears he will not last the night, but he doesn't see the point of calling a doctor. He puts an album on the record player whose scratches indicate that he has heard it more than once or twice, but this gap he'll have no trouble filling, he pours a generous amount of brandy, falls asleep surprisingly easily and after an hour or two wakes up with a shout that he couldn't complete in his dream. The dogs are barking on the platform in a foreign language. That same night Franz Kafka died.

Immigrants

Again they put the old and scratchy album on the record player. "Sometimes I look at you, in your sleep... maybe this is the rain... that hid the rain in your dreams." The engines are silent—it seems that the spaceship just spins lazily on its axis. Like they read in the guidebooks, the farther they get from the Earth, the more often they dream the same dream. Where the engines growl. Where the nameless baby cries. From the window they can once again see the silhouette of a plane tree and the rain of so many stars. The halfway point, once again, seems within reach.

Ars Poetica, Etc.

After the suicide of another senior lecturer in the literature department at the university in the south (the third such case in a two-month period of time), the police entered the picture. Their main suspicion in the murders—this was how the suicides were now openly known—fell on a perennial doctoral candidate, who after ten years had not managed to finish (or start, in fact) the work of his doctorate, which was a study entitled (promisingly, it must be acknowledged): "Ars Poetica of Suicide Notes in Eighteenth-Century French Novels." Two weeks ago, when I encountered him by chance in the cafeteria, he seemed defeated, a shadow of his former self. He told me that none of his interrogators understood anything about literature (except, perhaps, for one dark-eyed policewoman, who plays with her hair whenever he mentions the epistolary novels of de Laclos); to incriminate him they even invite a special expert in poisons from the city; it appears to him that the fate of his academic career—in a hoarse whisper he admitted that he knew this even before the sad affair befell him—has been decided. The day before yesterday, by contrast, I met him at the library exit: his eyes were joyful, he was even clean-shaven. In his hand he carried a botanical dictionary with wild lilacs illustrating its covers. "I—to the police" he declared enthusiastically. Later I learned that he had sent university officials a letter informing them of his abandonment of his doctoral work; that he had indeed met with one of his interrogators outside of working hours; that he had begun, as is required in these situations, to write a detective novel, and so on.

Painting Without a Painting

Because there is no story without a story: On a domestic flight in the United States I sat next to a freckled woman of about forty-five, who put aside a book that she'd opened to the place where a cloth ribbon stitched to the binding rested, and told me that she always knew, since she was a girl in a Minnesota more frozen than any memory, what would be the next song on the radio—and sometimes, if she tried, she correctly guessed the song after that ("But I never managed," she said, "to predict more than two songs.") Later, somewhere over Nevada, she also told me about her family: Her daughter, whom she was on her way to see, had adorable twins and a house in Orlando. Her oldest son was on his second marriage... He was a lawyer in a Washington firm. (Her husband, on the other hand, had been out of work for six years, but there was always hope, right?) "The last time I read this book," she said before she went back to the protected space of reading at a height of 30,000 feet above the ground, "It turned out that the thief who stole the painting from the Museum of Modern Art is the painter who painted the painting. The detective who solves the case again senses that something is missing. The painting is never found. After a few years in jail, the painter returns to the scene of the crime, to see what hangs in its place."

Untitled. Flood

Now they must also install bookshelves in the third room, which the old blueprints, from the time when they had just renovated the apartment, indicate is a nursery.

Untitled. Sisyphus Attempts Suicide

Like the last time, the stone that rolled down the mountain stopped exactly halfway down. In the sky, as though to emphasize the vividness of the photograph, circles a flock of crows.

The Second Minotaur

Plutarch gives us another version of the story of Theseus in the labyrinth. The minotaur speaks to Theseus before Theseus kills him. He says another minotaur is in the labyrinth, but the skein of thread in Theseus's hand is not enough for him to find it and return. "Thus the complexity of the labyrinth," writes Plutarch. "But it doesn't matter," says the minotaur. "After you kill me, the second minotaur will also die. He will die of loneliness." Plutarch adds that Theseus slaughters the minotaur without blinking an eye and leaves the labyrinth. But because of his excessive pride, he cannot take credit for the death of the second minotaur—when he returns, he refuses to raise his ship's white sail, the one meant to be a signal to his father, Aegeus, that his mission was successful. Here Plutarch's story merges with the other versions of the return of Theseus. His father sees the ship's black sail and hurls himself from the cliff, into the sea that has ever since been called the Aegean.

Metafiction

The ghost was still breastfeeding.

How to Arrange Your Lover's Library

This was only a rather old dictionary with a ragged cover. He had no idea that for half a year the folded scrap of paper in D's handwriting had been hidden inside.

They used to use the dictionary to play a game they invented. When it was his turn, he looked in the dictionary for an archaic and unfamiliar word and paired it with a definition that sounded logical. He presented the word to D along with the definition he invented and the definition from the dictionary.

For example: *Empasm*: "A sudden, intense, and sympathetic feeling " or "A perfumed powder once used in healing." She would have to choose which of the definitions was true. If she answered correctly—sometimes she simply knew the meaning of the word—it was her turn.

He leafed through the dictionary and remembered with a smile how she once tried to deceive him and made up a word that didn't exist: "to rain continuously, to rain both day and night" or "one hundred seventy cubits, ten times an elephant's height."

The old dictionary stood to the right of one the spaces that opened up when she left. He had only meant to take it off of the shelf, to clear out a place for the new and used books he bought. He had already obtained copies of most of her books. "If only we could arrange it all differently," she wrote. "Like cummings' spring. Fraction of flower here, placing an inch there, and without breaking anything."

The Death of an Escape Artist

True Comics

Among the tourist guides to esoteric museums all over the world, one certainly must describe—beside the Museum of Antique Shoes in Barcelona, the Museum of Telephones in Budapest, and the Cat Museum in Amsterdam—the tiny exhibit space hidden in one of the alleyways off of the Maximilianstrasse in the Old City of Munich, entitled "The Museum of the German Houdini." Exhibited there is a collection of posters (many of them framed and hanging on the walls of the museum) that were circulated to promote performances by the well-known escape artist of the time, Yaakov Pinsky, a cousin of my great-grandfather on my mother's side. (On the back of the only photograph in our family album in which he appears is a notation of the date, September 6, 1928. The young man on the right is Yaakov, and on the left is my great-grandfather, Michael, who left Germany the same year because he caught the fever of Communism, but this is likely to turn into another story inside a story, exactly like the photo album that my great-grandfather holds in the picture of the two of them...)

It appears that he already adopted the stage name "The German Houdini" for his first appearances, in 1931. His last documented performance before the war took place at eight in the evening on April 2, 1935, in a theater in Baden-Baden (where he performed one of his famous escape routines: he was bound in a straitjacket and put inside a cage with a gorilla. The cage was covered with cloth and less than a minute later Yaakov sat free, legs crossed, a small glass of cognac in his hand and the giant ape lying at his side, bound hand and foot in the straitjacket. He was once interviewed by the local Munich newspaper and in response to the banal question of how he carried this out, his impudent reply was that it was possible to repeat this act with a slight reversal of roles, because the only thing that matters is who gets to the cage last). It's possible that the same year he appeared a few more times in Switzerland, after he managed to obtain forged documents and join the tour of a circus from Berlin. In 1938, at the age of thirty-four, he was arrested and sent to Buchenwald. Five years later he was transported to Auschwitz.

His history during the first years after the war is foggy; apparently he sailed to Palestine, but it's doubtful that he found an audience for his art there. And indeed, other newspaper clippings exhibited today in the museum in Munich indicate that in 1950 he returned to perform in the city of his birth. From locked steel boxes immersed in water, hands and feet in chains, he usually broke out with his mouth frothing with blood, as if implying to the applauding spectators that he had simply chewed through the metal handcuffs with his teeth.

In another place—or maybe only here—we find a description of one of the acts he used to perform as an appetizer: he would fold one of the posters that advertised his act lengthwise and then across and then again, and then again and again, lengthwise and across and again lengthwise, and again... he reached the limits of the paper: eight folds. Then he managed to nevertheless fold the poster one more time. Then he would spread out the folded poster completely and show the audience that everything that had been pictured and written there was now erased, as if his folding had simply turned the page blank.

His health deteriorated after an accident in May of 1959. He tripped suddenly over a hole dug in the street and fell under a streetcar. As the end nears, the freedom of an artist grows stronger. He remained paralyzed from the waist down, but insisted, after two nightmarish months in the hospital, on returning to the stage and performing the complicated escape act until his last days. On the posters for his final performances, he is pictured with his torso bare, muscular and dark, sitting in a wheelchair, beneath a giant headline with his new stage name, "The Crippled Houdini."

On the afternoon of June 8, 1961, he fainted in the middle of a rehearsal and was hospitalized. He refused outright to be injected with morphine; but nevertheless the shot was administered at eight-thirty in the evening, after which he again lost consciousness; we can assume that he was spared another long detoxification from pain; before midnight he died in the hospital, hemorrhaging from his liver. Carved on his gravestone in the Jewish cemetery of Munich, as instructed in his will, is his real name, Yaakov Pinsky, and the names of his parents, Hannah and Abraham.

More Imaginary Photos

An old man rearranges his library. A couple lies in bed, on their backs, and shares a cigarette. A swimmer on a diving board spots an airplane from the corner of his eye. A father tells his son before bedtime: "Imagine that! The elephant turned into a moth..." An old man rearranges a library, and can no longer remember why. On most of the world's windows flow veins of rain.

Ithaca in the Rain. The Rain in Auschwitz

Once upon a time there was a writer who published a memoir of his childhood in Buchenwald. This was the first time that he'd written about the Holocaust. All his life he wrote love stories (and in all of his love stories it rained endlessly, on almost every page, so that it was possible to close the book and still smell the odor of damp earth from within the leather binding, but this is another matter). Only after a few years, on his deathbed, he admitted that the whole story was nothing more than a fabrication. In those days he was not in Buchenwald, but in Auschwitz. And only for a year.

Love's Spare Parts

This is also not a story because it is a love story: Research has proven that people who speak Semitic languages (Hebrew and Arabic, for example) don't forget them after a stroke. Because the database of these languages is distributed between the two sides of the brain. This phenomenon also happens to angels—unless they have a stroke while in midair, and then they are not sure how to land. The man in the bar who told me these facts said that tomorrow he was going to buy an electric wheelchair for his wife. She had muscular dystrophy. He found a place that sold them with a lifetime guarantee.

The Wise Painter

And in that rainy kingdom lives a painter who only paints on hundred-year-old canvases, which are preserved in some workshops in that rainy kingdom. When he has used up these canvases, he will paint over them from the beginning.

On the Homeless, Heading Home

In Denver I saw a homeless man with a suitcase walking slowly from nowhere to nowhere. A few meters behind him, a torn plastic bag floated above the sidewalk. Wherever he turned—the plastic bag turned behind him. I once read about a similar incident that happened to Genghis Khan, but in his case it wasn't a plastic bag, but a cloud in the heavens.

On the Poetics of Footnotes

I was once invited to teach creative writing in a mental hospital. To convince me that it wouldn't be the end of the world, the doctor who invited me said that the previous year a poet taught the mental patients. "Now it all makes sense," I said. And indeed, after the first lesson I was committed involuntarily. They told me: "We'll release you when you write a novel." In the beginning I excelled at hiding the pills they gave me under my tongue, later I went back to believing in the doctrines of Marx and Engels, and in the end I gave up and began to write as though possessed by a demon. In any event, this isn't a true story.

On How to Not Kill a Spider

Cover the spider with a small, shallow dish, such as a soap dish. Tilt the soap dish a little, and slip a piece of paper under it. Take the paper covered with the soap dish to a window. Carefully lift the soap dish and blow on the spider until it slides from the paper and out the window. Seventy percent of people who commit suicide by jumping from a high floor—I learned this from a study—feel remorse on their way down. I have no idea who volunteered to participate in this study, and at exactly which stage on the way down it was conducted. Aside from the method described here, there are many other ways to leave a small impression on the world.

A Compendium of Most Snowflakes

The last man in the world wrote the last haiku in the world.

Acknowledgments

My deepest gratitude to Dalit Lev, Becka McKay, Moshe Ron, Tal Nitzan, Adam Rovner, Rana Werbien, Hilary Plum, Marina Grosslerner, Tamar Marin, Juliana Spear, Tomer Lichtash, Pam Thompson, and Shui Tzui (and again the time traveler fell in love with you at first sight).